Ju
F
G43   Ginsburg, Marvell.
b   The tattooed Torah.

Ju
F
G43   Ginsburg, Marvell.
b   The tattooed Torah.

Temple Israel Library
Minneapolis, Minn.

Please sign your full name on the above
card.

Return books promptly to the Library or
Temple Office.

Fines will be charged for overdue books
or for damage or loss of same.

DEMCO

THE TATTOOED TORAH

by Marvell Ginsburg

illustrated by Jo Gershman

UNION OF AMERICAN HEBREW CONGREGATIONS
New York, New York

In memory of Stanley
and to my children
who have always encouraged me
and to all children everywhere
with hope for peace

Feldman Library

The Feldman Library Fund was created in 1974 through a gift from the Milton and Sally Feldman Foundation. The Feldman Library Fund, which provides for the publication by the UAHC of selected outstanding Jewish books and texts, memorializes Sally Feldman, who in her lifetime devoted herself to Jewish youth and Jewish learning. Herself an orphan and brought up in an orphanage, she dedicated her efforts to helping Jewish young people get the educational opportunities she had not enjoyed.

In loving memory of my beloved wife Sally
"She was my life, and she is gone;
She was my riches, and I am a pauper."

"Many daughters have done valiantly,
but thou excellest them all."

Milton E. Feldman

This is the story of a little tattooed Torah. It was always little but not always tattooed. Here is how it became tattooed.

Many, many years ago, before you were born, when your grandparents were children, Little Torah lived in a handsome, wooden Aron Kodesh that had a velvet, purple parochet.

It was in an old, beautiful synagogue in the city of Brno in Czechoslovakia. In the Aron

Kodesh, with Little Torah, were many big Torahs wearing soft, velvet mantles of scarlet,
purple, and blue. Little Torah was very proud
to be there with them. Some big Torahs had
silver crowns. Little Torah thought they looked
like kings and queens. Other big Torahs had

silver bells that made a gentle, jingling sound. It was a silvery, sweet song when they were taken out of the ark on Shabbat mornings and on holidays. Oh, how they jingled when the grown-ups hugged them lovingly in their arms marching in the Torah procession, singing Hebrew songs.

Little Torah was very proud. Every Bar Mitzvah child wanted to carry Little Torah in the procession and read his Torah portion from it. Shabbat after Shabbat, holiday after holiday, year after year, Little Torah was held by a child marching in the procession.

One day everything changed. Little Torah shivered. It heard a different kind of marching sound. It was not the sound of Jewish people marching into synagogue on Shabbat. It was not the sound of Jewish people marching into synagogue on a holiday. It was not the sound of children and grown-ups marching in the Torah service procession. It was loud, mean marching, with loud, mean talk.

Nazi soldiers were marching into Little Torah's town—into Brno! Their evil leader, Hitler, had started a war against the whole world. They marched into the synagogue. They ripped open the parochet. They pulled down the big Torahs. They threw off the silver crowns and jingling bells. Then they grabbed Little Torah.

They didn't hug and kiss Little Torah. They didn't hold it gently in their arms and march happily and sing Hebrew songs. They were rough. They threw Little Torah on a pile of Torahs in the back of a dark truck. They threw the crowns and bells in a sack with other crowns, breastplates, and Torah pointers. The truck rumbled out of the town. Little Torah was terrified. How could anyone do such a terrible thing to Torahs! The Nazi soldiers driving the truck laughed about closing up the synagogue —about taking the silver crowns and bells!

Little Torah cried.

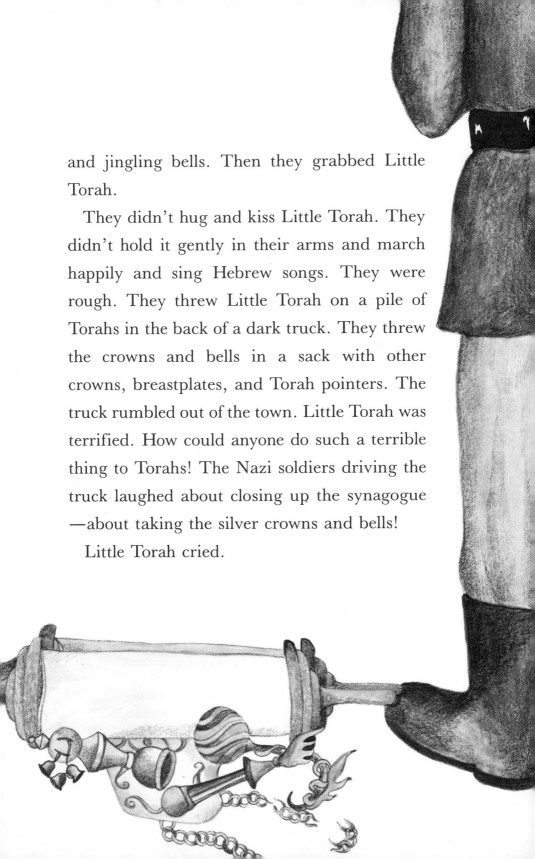

Many hours later, the truck stopped in the city of Prague. The Nazi soldiers opened the back of the truck. They took all the Torahs into a large warehouse where other Torahs from all over Czechoslovakia were stored.

"We're getting rid of the Jews, forever," they jeered. "But we'll keep their Torahs for souvenirs. Ha, Ha! We'll tattoo a number on each one. And we'll put the numbers in our record book so we'll know from which town they came."

That's just what they did. They put numbers on the bottom of one of the wooden rollers of each Torah scroll. Then, to make matters worse, they tied a wire with a swastika tag onto the other roller!

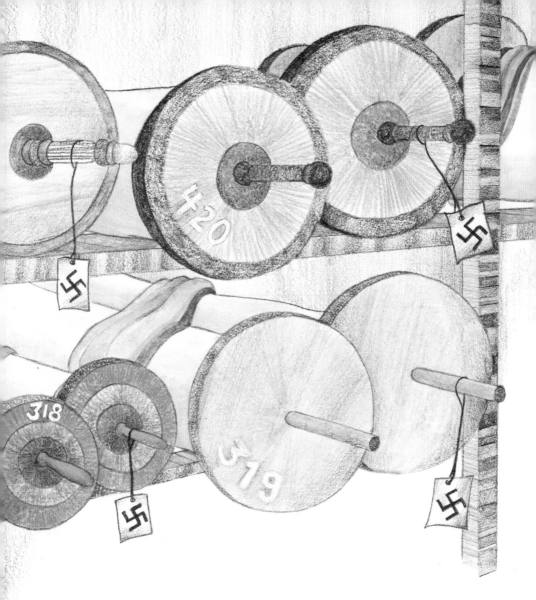

Little Torah was very angry. "They have no right to tattoo a Torah! A Torah is the most precious possession of the Jewish people and the whole world!"

A Nazi soldier grabbed the little Torah and put a number on the bottom of one of its wooden rollers and wired a swastika tag to the other. Then Little Torah was put on a rough wooden shelf with all the other Torahs.

Little Torah was very sad.

Day after day, Little Torah heard the Nazi soldiers march into the warehouse, saying mean things and bringing in fresh truckloads of Torahs. Day after day, numbers were tattooed on the Torahs and swastika tags were wired onto them. Day after day, numbers were put in the record book.

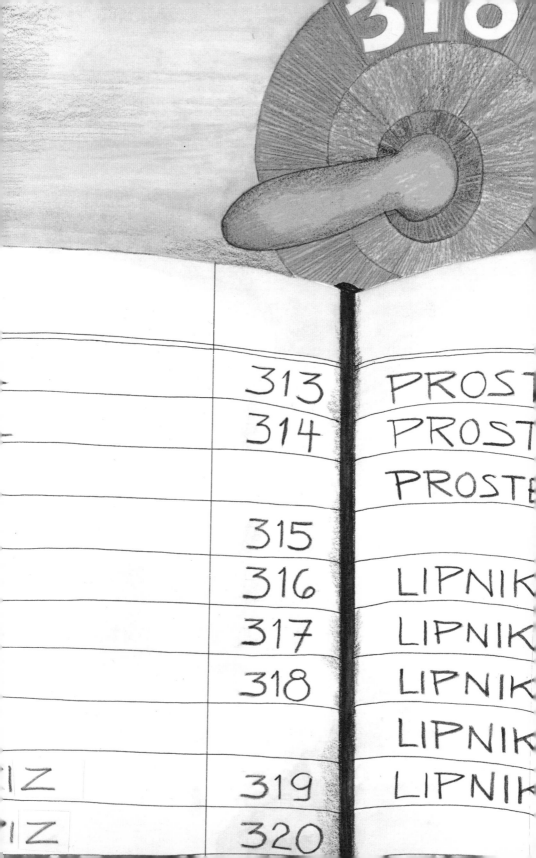

318

| | 313 | PROST
| | 314 | PROST
| | | PROSTE
| | 315 |
| | 316 | LIPNIK
| | 317 | LIPNIK
| | 318 | LIPNIK
| | | LIPNIK
| IZ | 319 | LIPNIK
| IZ | 320 |

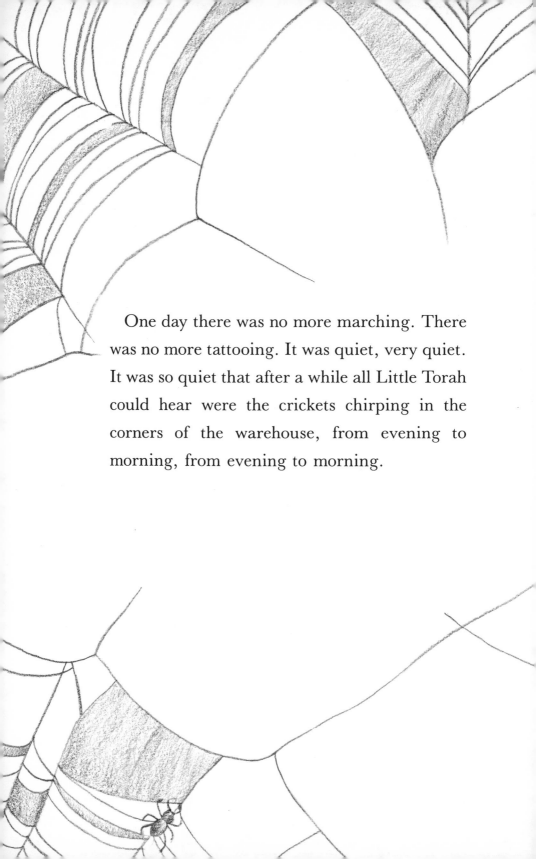

One day there was no more marching. There was no more tattooing. It was quiet, very quiet. It was so quiet that after a while all Little Torah could hear were the crickets chirping in the corners of the warehouse, from evening to morning, from evening to morning.

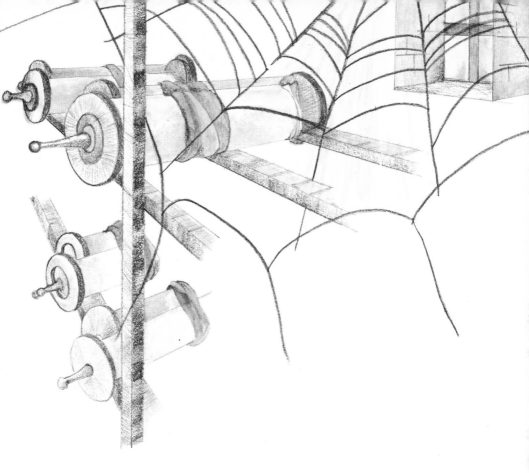

Then it was a new day and the war was over.
Friendly soldiers, called the Allied Forces, had
won the war against the Nazis. The Nazis were
gone from Brno. They were gone from Prague.
But Little Torah still remained in the warehouse, because there were no Jews left in Brno
to take Little Torah home.

Many years after the war ended, an American Jewish man named Arthur Weil was asked by his children's school principal to find a small Torah light enough for young children to hold during services.

After searching and asking where he could find such a Torah, Mr. Weil finally went to Prague. There, he was taken to the warehouse where all the Torahs from the synagogues all over Czechoslovakia had been stored by the Nazis.

In the warehouse in front of him were hundreds of Torahs on rough wooden shelves—1,500 of them. These Torahs were not dressed in beautiful velvet mantles of scarlet, purple, or blue. They were wrapped in old, spotted rags. But, worst of all, each Torah had a wire with a swastika tag tied to one roller.

Mr. Weil went closer to look at the Torahs. He saw that each one had a number tattooed on it as well. The tears began to roll down Mr. Weil's cheeks and he started to sob. He stood there crying for a long time.

"Torahs with swastika tags! How could anyone do this to Torahs? I must do something to get them out of here."

Mr. Weil then flew to London where he went to Westminster Synagogue. He told the people about the Torahs in the warehouse.

"We must save those Torahs," he told them. "We must take off those swastika tags. Torahs belong in synagogues, not in a warehouse!"

The people shouted, "Yes, yes. We must save the Torahs!"

And they did. They all gave money until they had enough to put all 1,500 Torahs on airplanes and fly them to London to be cleaned and repaired—all 1,500 including Little Torah.

That's when Mr. Weil discovered and chose Little Torah, the small Torah light enough for young children to hold during services. He naturally took off the wire holding the swastika tag. He also had a red velvet mantle made especially to fit Little Torah; and, embroidered in gold, on the front, were a Jewish star and the word "Zachor"—remember. Now, again, Little Torah began to feel proud.

Mr. Weil looked at the tattooed number on one of the wooden rollers of Little Torah, then in the record book which showed the town from which Little Torah came—Brno.

"Oh, what a wonderful Torah," exclaimed Mrs. Weil when she saw it. "It is just the right size for the children to hold. They will love it."

"Yes," agreed Mr. Weil. "Now we must build a special Aron Kodesh and a special parochet, the right size for our little Torah." And that's just what they did.

When the new Aron Kodesh and parochet were finished, the school principal invited all the children, their parents, grandparents, and teachers to a special service in honor of their new little Torah. Little Torah shivered with joy as it was taken from the ark and everyone marched in the procession. Little Torah was handed to the youngest child who led them in the joyous march around the school building singing, oh, so happily, "Torah, Torah, Torah, Torah, Torah, Torah, Torah tzivah lanu Moshe." (The Torah was commanded to us by Moses.)

When the procession returned to the sanctuary, Little Torah was unrolled and two children read from the portion of the week.

Little Torah was bursting with pride. What a wonderful, wonderful day—even better than a Bar Mitzvah.

At the conclusion of the service, when Little Torah was back in the ark, Mr. Weil told everyone the story of the little tattooed Torah. Little Torah sighed with happiness listening from the new Aron Kodesh. "And now children," Mr. Weil concluded, with tears in his eyes, "the little tattooed Torah is yours. May it dwell forever in this house of love and learning." With tears streaming down their cheeks, children and grown-ups alike softly said, "Amen."

Temple Israel
Minneapolis, Minnesota

IN HONOR OF THE 90TH BIRTHDAY OF

ROSE SCHLEIFF

FROM

RALEIGH KARATZ